T0197521

The Unique Unicorn

Adryanna Cottemond
Illustrated by Chantalyra Cottemond

To order additional copies of this book, contact:
Xlibris
844-714-8691
www.Xlibris.com
Orders@Xlibris.com

ISBN: Softcover   978-1-6641-9782-4
         Hardcover   978-1-6641-9783-1
         EBook   978-1-6641-9781-7

Print information available on the last page

Rev. date: 10/29/2021

The Unique Unicorn

Adryanna Cottemond

Once upon a time, there was a little unicorn named Lavender who lived in a magical town called Snow Crystal. Everyone in Snow Crystal had magical powers, except for Lavender.

One day, Lavender cried to her mother, "When will I get my magic like all the other unicorns? Everyone makes fun of me," Lavender cried.

Lavender's mother replied, "Be patient, dear, your magic will come in due time. Besides, there is nothing wrong with being a little unique."

As Grandma Sparkle entered the room, she asked, "Lavender, have you experienced any changes yet?"

"Not yet, Grandma Sparkle. What's wrong with me? I just don't understand why I don't have any powers," Lavender cried.

Grandma Sparkle looked at Lavender and said, "Lavender, I would like for you to take a little journey through Crystal Forest with your friends Lollipop and Sunshine to meet a fairy named Petal Rose. Perhaps, Petal Rose can help you find your magic powers."

Lavender told Lollipop and Sunshine about the journey through Crystal Forest to meet the fairy and they both were excited to go.

As the three unicorns flew over the clouds to enter the forest, a gust of wind came from behind the clouds. It was TuTu, the twirling troll.

"Where do you three think you are going, flying over my clouds?" she said twirling around and around.

"We are going to see the fairy Petal Rose, so she can help Lavender find her magical powers," replied Sunshine.

The twirling troll began to laugh. "Ha ha ha ha! You are actually going to go into that forest? Ha ha! Crystal Forest! Ha ha! Have you guys lost your minds?" stated the twirling troll in tears from laughing so hard.

Lollipop replied, "Ha ha! What is so funny about going into the forest?"

"You really don't know, do you?" stated the troll.

"Know what?" the three unicorns yelled in unison at the troll.

"Well, since you want to know, there is a dragon deep into the forest named Dragon Dracon. She is the last dragon of the Dracon family. She is the queen of the forest. No one has entered the forest for thousands of years.

"I am going to let all of you pass my clouds for free this time, so I can have an interesting story to tell about the three unicorns that never returned from Crystal Forest."

As Lavender, Lollipop, and Sunshine flew over the clouds and entered the forest, they admired the beauty of Crystal Forest as they landed to the ground.

While looking around, Sunshine could see darkness throughout the forest underneath the beauty with her X-ray vision as she shed the light of sunshine through her eyes.

Looking, listening, and roaming through the forest very carefully, the unicorn heard a cry for help. The closer they got, the louder the cry was heard.

"It sounds like it's near the waterfall," Lavender said.

"I don't see anything but a fish tail," replied Lollipop.

"Look to the right," yelled Sunshine.

"It's a mermaid," whispered Lavender.

While moving closer, the unicorns noticed two mermaids, but one was injured. The three approaching unicorns startled the mermaids.

Lavender said, "We heard your cry for help as we were passing through the forest. I am Lavender, and these are my friends, Lollipop and Sunshine."

"I am Ula and this is my friend Lyris."

"What happened to Lyris?" asked Sunshine.

Ula explained, "We were attacked by Dragon Dracon." With tears of sorrow in her eyes, she cried and stated, "This is all my fault. If only we had stayed underwater, but no, I just had to see the famous dragon. Now my friend is hurt and no one knows where we are."

As Lollipop approached the injured mermaid, her pink horn began to sparkle. The mermaid Lyris was beginning to heal, for Lollipop had the power to heal.

"Thank you," cried Ula.

Once the mermaid had awakened, both mermaids asked, "Why are the three of you here in Crystal Forest?"

Lavender replied, "We are here to see the fairy Petal Rose, to see if she can help me find my magic powers."

Ula asked, "Are you sure you want to continue your journey knowing what that vicious dragon can do to you?"

"If my friends will continue with me, then yes, I would like to finish this journey," replied Lavender.

Lollipop and Sunshine replied, "We started this together and we will end this together. That's what friends are for. Let's do this!"

As the unicorns walked away, Ula and Lyris yelled, "Be careful, goodbye!"

The unicorns continued their trail to find the fairy. Lavender's crystal horn began to change colors. One minute it was purple, then it was pink and blue, and now it's yellow, Lollipop asked, "Lavender, are you okay?"

"Yes, why do you ask?" Lavender replied.

"Because your horn is changing colors like a rainbow," Lollipop replied, laughing.

"It's only changing into four colors," Sunshine whispered.

"Oh my goodness! What is happening to me!" yelled Lavender.

"Probably magic," replied Sunshine and Lollipop.

"What kind of magic is this changing colors," cried Lavender.

"Wait! Listen," whispered Sunshine as she used her X-ray vision to look around. "She is almost near us!" yelled Sunshine.

"Who?" replied Lavender.

"It's the dragon!" screamed Sunshine. "Ruuuuuun! No! Fly!"

"Why! Either way we are in danger!" screamed Lollipop. "So we might as well fight. I am not afraid. I will slay Queen Dracon today!" yelled Lollipop.

As the big, red, and vicious, fire-breathing dragon approached, Lavender's crystal horn began to change colors rapidly. The three friends stood side by side to face the dragon. Through the X-ray vision, Sunshine didn't see darkness in the forest anymore, Lollipop's horn began to sparkle, which meant someone needed healing. Lavender began speaking to the fire-breathing dragon as hot blazing balls of fire roared out of the Queen's mouth.

"We come in peace," yelled Lavender. "We are only here to see the fairy Petal Rose." Queen Dracon had a quick flashback of something her father told her many years ago about a unique unicorn with a crystal horn.

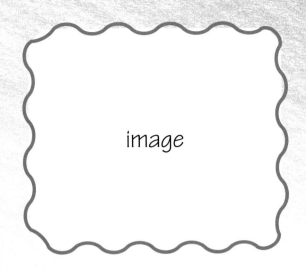

With smoke blowing from her nose, the dragon yelled, "It is you, the unique unicorn with the crystal horn that changes colors." The three unicorns looked surprised. The dragon explained, "Many years ago, my father told me a story about a unique unicorn with a crystal horn that changes to four meaningful colors --purple for loyalty, yellow for friendship, blue for peace, and pink for love --will show up and restore friendship throughout the forest."

The unicorns asked, "Will you take us to the fairy Petal Rose?"

"Sure," the dragon replied.

As Dragon Dracon walked through the forest with the three unicorns, the other animals began to whisper, as they see the unique unicorn Lavender stroll through the forest with the dragon. Everyone then began to realize that it wasn't just a myth about the unique unicorn. The closer the unicorns and the dragon got to Petal Rose the more the forest smelled like roses. Lavender said, "Look everyone, it is raining pixie dust. We must have made it to Petal Rose." The pink petals of a rose began to open up and a kind sweet voice said "Yes, you have made it to the Petal Rose. No need to introduce yourself. We have been expecting you Lavender for many years. You want me to help you find your powers?" Petal Rose asked.

"Yes," Lavender replied.

"Truth is, Lavender, you don't have any powers," Petal Rose explained. "You are that special little unique unicorn that spreads love and friendship from within. Your colorful crystal horn symbolizes love, loyalty, peace, and friendship no matter how different you are. Today, Queen Dracon was released from her Darkness, her broken heart was healed, and she was no longer alone, thanks to the unique unicorn and her two friends."

Lavender and her two friends Sunshine and Lollipop were at a loss for words. All of the animals in Crystal Forest began to fellowship; and friendship was restored back throughout the forest.

Once Lavender made it back home, she thanked Grandma Sparkle for sending her on a journey to see the fairy Petal Rose.

"I learned today that it is okay to be unique. Everyone is special in their own way, no matter how different they are. With or without magic powers."

Printed in the United States
by Baker & Taylor Publisher Services